# Scamper, A Cat

# And Other Stories for Grown Ups

## By

## Margot Fritz

G

This book is a work of fiction. Places, events, and situations in this story are purely fictional. Any resemblance to actual persons, living or dead, is coincidental.

ISBN: 1-4033-8214-X (e-book)
ISBN: 1-4033-8215-8 (Paperback)

This book is printed on acid free paper.

1stBooks - rev. 01/16/03

# TABLE OF CONTENTS

# PREFACE

When I look back over my life (and at this writing I am 68), I see that at critical times there has been a cat person around. Soon after my parents divorce when I was seven my mother got me a kitten and named him Domino because he had a black mask. Domino was my friend and companion at a time that was lonely and difficult for me. He was a most adaptable cat - as happy in a New York apartment as at our home in Mamaroneck where he could roam free, something he often did on the marshes behind the house when he would accompany me on my solitary walks. In the New York apartments we lived in we would play chase up and down the halls. He liked to hide under the skirt of my dressing table, making running forays to bat me around the ankles before disappearing under the dressing table skirt again.

During the years of my marriage when I was absorbed in the tasks of running a household, parenting three children and working part time cats came and they went, but they were peripheral to my life. It wasn't until after my divorce after 22 years of marriage that I found myself with another cat who would become important to me. That cat was Pippin - the central character of "Love Story."

What I have come to know is that the animal creatures we call our 'pets' have a meaning and significance in our lives that can equal and sometimes exceed the importance of our human relationships. As the pace of life in America has become increasingly frantic the toll it has taken has accelerated as well. Two out of three marriages now end in divorce. The latest US Census reveals that there are more people in this country living alone than at any previous time in our history. My hunch is that for millions of my fellow Americans this condition of 'alone' includes a cat or a dog, that in fact these people are not really alone, but are, like me, in a relationship with an animal person.

I think it is often hard for people to acknowledge the importance of an animal in their life. We discount the relationship, to ourselves and to others. But I have noticed that the language people use to talk about their 'pets' in unguarded moments reveals a depth of feeling and dependence that is surprising.

We all need love and acceptance and someone to share our most private moments with. It is not always possible to have a human relationship in our lives that will provide us with that support. Our animal relationships can fill this void.

So - without embarrassment I dedicate this book to all those who, like me, have a place in their hearts for love of a cat.

# Pippin: A Love Story

# LOVE STORY

This is a love story, but like millions of my fellow Americans who share this love with me, it is one I am a little embarrassed about. Like them I suspect that others may think this love a little unnatural - even deviant. So, in an effort to hide our true feelings we make light of our love, joke about it and hope we haven't been found out.

My story did not begin as a love story. Quite the contrary. I was determined to get rid of the party as quickly and expeditiously as possible. It happened this way. I woke one morning and, propped on my elbows, half awake and still in bed something zigged past my line of vision. I did not quite believe my eyes. Was that a tail? There were at that time, no tails in my household. The last tail had departed years ago when the family cat simply did not reappear after being put out one evening. So to whom did this tail belong?

In pursuit of the answer I arose, donned bathrobe and staggered wearily to the kitchen there to be greeted by a ridiculous ball of black and orange fluff attempting to call itself a kitten. "Adam" I yelled, "what is a kitten doing in this house?" From somewhere towards the front of the house came the reply in my son's unmistakable basso profundo, "Pipe down Mom - you're gonna wake the neighbors." My youngest son, at the time only 6'1' (he still had another inch to go) and 185 pounds, loomed into view.

"See Mom what happened is —"

"Adam, I don't care what happened, I don't want a cat. Period."

3

"Mom, you gotta listen to me. She's abused. No really. Look at her here, see, between her shoulder blades - "

With this my son scooped up the kitten and held it - her - under my nose and parted the fur at the nape of her neck.

"See. No hair. Know why? Because Steve's idiot brother likes to pull her hair out and listen to her yowl. He's sick, and I just couldn't stand it so I took her. Please Mom, you gotta take care of her. She'll die if you don't."

My son Adam has always had my number. My third, and last, child, he was the delight of my life from the moment of his arrival and for all his 17 years he had known just how to 'work' me.

At that moment I could not muster whatever it would have taken by way of true grit to evict the small, hapless animal who was mewing piteously and cowering in front of the washing machine on the service porch. I bent down to pick her up and that served as my final capitulation although I did not know it at the time.

I named her "Pippin" and she became my best - and at times my only friend. My 'baby' left home shortly afterwards and as my ex and I had recently separated I found myself alone for the first time in my adult life. My life was full at the time and as a result being alone was not the nightmare that it often is for newly and about to be divorced, women. I rather enjoyed it. My house was small and for the first time since we'd bought it I felt comfortable in it. There we were, just me and Pippin.

She was a small, dainty cat, a short haired tortoise shell with black and orange fur except for two white paws and a white tummy. She had a small marking of orange fur over one eye which gave her an asymmetrical look as though she was perpetually puzzled about something. Despite the teasing and mishandling she had received as a kitten she socialized easily and sat happily in all my visitors laps with or without invitation.

In the months and years we shared our lives we became very dependent on each other. Just how dependent was not brought home to me until one rainy March evening when I came home from work, opened my front door expecting to see her, tail up and back arched in greeting on the arm of the white chair by the front door. When she was not there I was only mildly concerned. She was probably asleep in the middle of my bed. But she wasn't. Nor was she in the kitchen, nor did she come flying over the back fence and across the back yard in response to my call. The night slowly began to assume a nighmare quality. Where was she? Had the rain found her in illicit activity in a neighbor's garage and had the weight of rain on the garage door caused it to close, trapping her inside? I called her periodically over the course of that evening but when she hadn't returned by midnight I went to bed and slept a restless, uncomfortable sleep knowing her soft furry presence was not beside me. Next morning I called the office and told them Pip was missing and that I had to look for her. Cat lovers all, the staff understood. I combed the neighborhood, calling, calling. I even went to the house of the Witch of Westchester, a horrid old woman named Lelo who collected cats, her own and other people's, under the misguided assumption that other people were incapable of loving cats as much as she did so she would intervene and 'save' the poor animal. Pippin was not at Lelo's. I went to work feeling awful; carrying a stone in the pit of my stomach, certain that she had been stolen, was lying dead in a gutter, or dying of slow starvation trapped in someone's garage.

By the evening of the second day I had called her and cried in despair so many times, driven the streets around my house so often looking and calling I was sure everyone in Westchester knew I'd lost her. One of my co-workers created a poster on her computer offering a reward for anyone who could find her and I papered Westchester with them and waited for the call that never came. A trip to the pound yielded nothing and made me feel worse for having to look among all those lost and wretched creatures.

By evening of the third day I had to acknowledge that she was gone for good and with that recognition came another. I, who was wont to trumpet loudly that I didn't mind living alone proclaiming to anyone who would listen, "I don't need anyone else! I'm just fine on my own thank you!" I, the great Miss Independence, was a fraud.

Like hell I didn't need anybody. Who was Pippin if not somebody? Who was Pippin if not the one I counted on to be there at the door to greet me - to share my lonely evenings of TV, curled happily in my lap - to offer me the comfort of her furry, warm body nestled into mine in bed and without whom I slept a miserable sleep. Who was I kidding? Without Pippin I was a mess.

I remember that night so well. It had rained on and off all day and the house was cold when I got home. I had turned on the heat, made some dinner which I wasn't hungry for, watched the evening news and was sitting on the couch in the living room looking at a magazine and trying not to think about the fact that she was gone.

I was aware of a heavy, tight feeling in my body, a sadness beyond tears.

Suddenly my head jerked up, listening. There it was again; the smallest meow. "God! It can't be. I'm imagining it. That's not what I heard." But it came again. I rushed to the kitchen which seemed to be where this tiny sound was emanating from. Then out into the night to stand in the driveway beside the kitchen thinking perhaps it had come from under the house. I heard it again, this time louder, and now I was sure. It was her - it had to be her - but where in god's name was she? I ran back into the house and called my next door neighbor, Pat, who had gone searching with me when I combed the neighborhood. She came immediately and we both stood in the driveway, listening and she corroborated what I had heard; it was definitely a cat's meow. But where? Pat was about to go under the house through the crawl space when suddenly there was a loud thump from the kitchen.

I rushed into the house and pulled open a cupboard below the kitchen counter where I kept mixing bowls and out stepped Pippin. She was in no hurry - not seemingly in need of food or water. Pat and I meanwhile were acting like maniacs jumping up and down with the cat in all four of our arms, laughing and crying and scolding Pippin even as we buried our faces in her fur, telling her she was a 'bad' 'wonderful' cat and asking her 'where have you been and why did you worry us so?'

She had simply been hibernating for three days in a safe, dark, quiet place. After all it was raining outside - why not? She had not made any mess; just curled in a corner of the cupboard behind the mixing bowls and gone to sleep.

In all we shared our lives for 14 years and when at last I was forced to put her to sleep I held her in my arms as her body stiffened with death and told her to wait for me, to be there when I get there because Heaven is not a place I can imagine without her.

So that's my love story. As I said it's one I share with millions of my fellow Americans many of whom feel a little foolish acknowledging the love that exists between them and whatever kind of 'pet' they live with and so deny it with embarrassed laughter and remarks intended to discount the authenticity of their feelings.

I have puzzled over why I loved Pippin so and what she meant in my life. What I have come to understand is that my love for her was as pure a love as I will ever know. A love untinged with fear, projections of ego, demands that will be denied, expectations that cannot be met. A simple love, a truthful love.

# Scamper, A Cat – A Personal Journal

# SCAMPER, A CAT
## A Personal Journal

In the early morning hours of August 24th, a coyote trotted across an empty feed lot in the small dairy town of Bell on the Olympic Peninsula. The moon was full and its light gave a silvery patina to everything it touched. The coyote was hungry. As it approached a large bush of tangled blackberry vines it saw something gleaming whitely in the moonlight just the other side of the blackberry brambles. It stopped and stood very still, then dropped into a half crouch and very slowly advanced on the bush keeping its eyes glued to the white patch glimmering in the moonlight. Slowly, very slowly it crept forward until it had a clear view through the blackberry branches. There, just the other side of the bush, was a cat. It was a brown and black striped tabby with a white chest and four white legs. The cat was intent on prey of its own, a mouse rustling in the long grasses just a few feet away. Suddenly the cat pounced and in the next instant the coyote pounced as well, grabbing the cat by the nape of its neck. The coyote gave the cat a quick, sharp shake and the cat's body went suddenly limp. Carrying its trophy the coyote headed across the feed lot to its den, the cat's body swaying slightly in its jaws.

*****

My earliest memories are not good ones. They are mostly of sounds. I hear a dog snarling and snapping, and hear my mother spitting and yowling, while beside me my siblings are making frightened mewing sounds. Then there is nothing. But the sounds stay with me.

The next thing I remember is being in a cage in a place with bright lights and dogs barking. To this day I detest the sound of a dog barking. Why do dogs have to be so noisy? I was in a place called a pet shop and apart from the dogs what I remember is that I was alone, that as I grew the cage became too small for me, and that I hated the smell of the place.

Because I had been so badly frightened as a very small kitten I was not very outgoing. Mostly I slept. I liked it best at night when the shop was closed and the lights were turned down. That was the happiest part of my day.

My lacklustre personality was not an asset. People came into the shop, often with their children, looking for a pet. They would walk right by my cage. The pet shop owner positioned my cage close to the front so people would see me in hopes that someone would want me. They didn't. Children sometimes tried to pull my fur or my tail through the bars of the cage and I would hiss at them and try to scratch their hands with my claws, which were getting sharper. This of course wouldn't do so the owner moved my cage to the back which suited me just fine.

My legs grew longer and I outgrew the cute, kitten phase. One night at closing time the owner passed by my cage, then stopped, came back and looked closely at me. "I don't think you're going to sell," she said. "I think you're headed for the pound kiddo."

I didn't know what the 'pound' was but her tone was not encouraging.

Two days later a woman came into the shop and asked if there were any kittens. The owner shook her head, then said, "But we have a very cute young male with tabby markings. Let me show you."

She led the woman to the back of the store and they stopped in front of my cage. I had been sleeping, but when they stopped in front of me I raised my head and looked at the woman. She was older, but not old if you know what I mean.

"He's got lovely markings on his face," she said. The pet shop owner sensing a sale was quick to agree.

"He's been wormed and treated for ear mites and he'll make a lovely pet," she said trying to be enthusiastic without overselling.

"How old is he?" the woman asked.

"About seven months."

"What's his story?"

I could see that the shop owner was uncomfortable with this question and I was curious as to what she'd tell the woman.

"Well," she began slowly, "it seems a dog killed his mother and ate his litter mates."

"My God. How awful," the woman said and I could tell she really did think it was awful.

Nobody said anything for several seconds and I fully expected that to be the end of it. But it wasn't.

"May I hold him?" the woman asked.

"He's a little skittish, but let's see," the pet shop owner said opening the door to my cage.

To this day I don't know why I didn't spit and try to scratch the woman as she reached out to pick me up. But I didn't. I was scared though and began to tremble all over.

"Poor thing," she said as she attempted to cradle me in her arms. "It's all right sweetheart. I'm not going to hurt you. It's all right."

Something in the sound of her voice and the assurance with which she held me gave me comfort and I didn't protest.

"I'll take him," she said. She handed him to the pet shop owner who put me in a cardboard carrying case and I listened while the woman and the owner concluded the sale. The woman got a discount on me because I wasn't a kitten. I cost fifteen dollars.

I wasn't at all sure what was going to happen to me next as I felt the box swaying when the woman picked it up and carried it to her car. I was still shaking sometime later when the car stopped. I was carried inside and the box was opened.

I sat up and looked around. The woman was sitting close by on a couch watching me. Suddenly I sprang from the box, tore around the end of the couch and hid behind it. The space between the wall and the couch was just big enough for me and it was dark as well.

"Ok. Hide. Stay there as long as you like," the woman said.

I stayed for the rest of the day, but by sundown I was starting to get really hungry. I didn't complain, but the woman seemed to know that I would be hungry. She put water and a dish of food down on some newspaper in front of the couch. Then she sat down and waited.

I really didn't want to come out with her sitting there, but hunger finally got the better of me and I emerged slowly, peering about me, poised to run back behind the couch at the slightest noise or suspicious movement.

The woman sat quietly watching.

I crept to the food dish and began to eat. I was intent on the food when I felt her stroking the back of my head with the backs of her fingers. I was too hungry to care and since it didn't hurt I let her do it.

I stayed behind the couch for several days. After the first two days I got bored and began to come out in order to have a look around. I had never been in a house before so everything was new to me.

The first time I went into the kitchen she was standing at the sink. She turned around and saw me and said, "Well hi there." I tore back to the living room and hid behind the sofa. She was laughing and I heard her say, "I've never seen anybody scamper so fast in my life." Then she said, "Scamper. That's what we'll call you. Scamper." And from then on that was my name.

Slowly, because she was so calm and didn't try to make me do anything, but just let me hide behind the couch and take my time, I began to feel less scared. I got bolder and began to explore my territory. I wasn't allowed outside which was probably a good thing as I might well have run in the street and gotten hit by a car. I learned that the woman's name was odd so I just called her "M" and since all she could hear is meow anyway it really didn't matter what I called her. The house was in a place called a suburb of a very large city called Los Angeles.

The house where we lived was small, but fine for just me and M. Since she was often gone during the day I was free to go anywhere I wanted and I discovered that it was possible to create a wonderful den underneath her bedspread. I'd butt the spread with my head until I'd made a sort of tunnel, then I'd jump up on the bed, under the spread, and curl up. It became my favorite place to be.

I stopped being afraid of M very quickly because she was so gentle with me. It was a strange sensation to trust someone. I could not ever remember trusting anyone. As far back as I could remember I had always been frightened.

One night when M got in bed she saw the lump under the comforter and she reached under and picked me up. I remember sort of hanging in mid-air over the bed. A moment's panic seized me that something bad was about to happen. Instead M put me under the covers and nestled me under her arm. She stroked my fur and murmured nonsense words to me and I found I liked being close to her and feeling the warmth of her body and smelling her smell.

Then a funny thing happened. She began to make a faint rumbling sound. I listened to it for several moments and it seemed there was something vaguely familiar about it. The next thing I knew I was making the same sound.

"Good boy," she said. "You're purring. That's a purr Scamp. You didn't know how did you old boy?"

I couldn't tell her that once a long time ago I might have known what purring was, but that too much had happened to me in between for me to remember that far back. From then on though I knew what purring was and whenever she'd do it I'd do it too and it seemed to make us both happy.

Once I'd discovered how warm and safe I felt under the covers at night that became my sleeping place. Sometimes it would be too hot to be under the covers so I'd curl up on top of the comforter but as close to M as possible. She loved to stroke my fur when she was falling asleep.

I don't know when I realized it, but one day it was just clear to me that my life had taken a very definite turn for the better. I wasn't scared any more. I knew that I was safe with M. I knew that she would take care of me. I still got scared when other people were around, and certain noises could still make me run for cover, but for the most part life was good and I was a happy cat.

Every now and then things happened which set me back and made me afraid all over again. Like the time M took me to the vet and left me. M explained in the car on the way to the vet's that it would only be for overnight. She said I wouldn't feel any pain and that she would come and get me the very next day. Once there, I got scared. It reminded me too much of the pet store. There was that awful smell, and dog's yapping, and I was in a cage again. I hid under the newspaper in the bottom of the cage and the vet's assistant had to put on heavy leather gloves to pick me up because I was so upset I would have scratched him badly. I was taken to a room and placed on a table. There were bright lights in the room which hurt my eyes. I felt a tiny prick and the next thing I knew I was back in the cage with no memory at all of what had happened. I slept and the next morning M was there with my cat carrier and we went home. I was sore when I walked for a couple of days, but after that I was fine.

I had been with M for several months when one sunny Saturday morning she said, "Let's try it Scamp. I'm going to let you go outdoors, but first I'm going to show you the cat door."

She picked me up and took me to the back door on the service porch. She put me down on the floor in front of the door and then she gently pushed a panel in the door which, when it swung open, revealed a driveway and a hedge. Wonderful smells wafted through the open space. I approached the door cautiously while she held the panel open. I poked my head out and since there didn't seem to be anything dangerous going on I jumped out the door onto the back stoop. M came outside with me and walked up a few steps to a patio where she sat down on a glider and waited to see what I would do.

I liked the feel of sunshine on my fur. Suddenly it seemed very good to be outdoors. My nose was picking up all sorts of smells too, including something faintly delicious that I later learned was mouse.

There was a fence around the small garden and I jumped up on it and looked down into the neighboring yard which was flat with a big, open grassy space in the middle and flower borders around the edge of the lawn. In one corner I saw something that interested me. I jumped down onto the grass and approached it. It was about the size of a shoe box and brown. I walked slowly all around it sniffing, hoping it was edible.

Then I heard M's voice. She had been watching me from the other side of the fence. "Scamper leave Pokey alone. He's not going to hurt you and you can't eat him." M subsequently explained to me that 'Pokey' was a desert tortoise.

As I moved off into the flower border and disappeared under a bush I heard M saying, "You're on your own now Scamp. Don't get into trouble."

From then on I could come and go as I pleased and that suited me perfectly. M put two collar tags on me - one for my rabies vaccination and one with my name, address and phone number on it. When I moved they made a chinking noise. When M called me if she could hear my tags she knew I was close by and she wouldn't worry about me. However I learned to move in such a way that they didn't make a sound when I was stalking.

Often when I caught something I would bring it into the bedroom. M got upset when she found these 'surprises' as she called them. Sometimes the mice were just stunned so I could play with them before killing and eating them. If M found one that was stunned she'd pick it up by its tail and take it outside to let it go. Then she'd make me stay in the house for a while. That made me mad, but there was nothing I could do about it.

If it was a bird I'd caught she'd say in her sternest voice, "Scamper. This is not ok. You are not to kill birds."

But I did anyway. I couldn't help it. Stalking, hunting, killing is just something cats do. We've been doing it for centuries so we could survive and even when we live with humans we must keep our skills up. The other thing that M didn't understand was that the bedroom was my den and that's why I brought my kills there. I tried to be patient with her, but I soon realized it was just one of those thing she'd never accept.

Apart from that though she seemed to understand me very well and we had a good life together in the small house in the suburb of the place called Los Angeles.

During the day, while she was gone, I would nap under the comforter on M's bed. Then I'd go outside for a while and roam the neighborhood just to see what was going on. I liked to sit in the middle of the grass yard next door with my paws tucked under me. There was lots of green open space around me so nothing could sneak up on me and I felt safe. Pokey and I became friends and the two of us spent many happy hours dozing in the sun.

M's friends often asked her about me and she would bring them to the door of the bedroom and point to the lump under the bedspread and say, "There he is. That's Scamp." It became something of a game with some of her friends to see if they could catch a glimpse of me. But I remained aloof. I didn't want to risk trying to get close to anyone else. M was all I needed.

I had been living with M for more than a year when something happened which was to change our lives. M got a phone call one day just after she got home from work. She was sitting on the bed using the bedside phone and I heard her say, "When?" And then, "Oh God." She didn't talk for quite a while and then she said, "Thank you, Peter. Thank you for all you've done for him. I know you loved him and I know you tried. You mustn't blame yourself. It's not your fault."

After she hung up she just sat on the edge of the bed, not moving. Then she started to cry only it wasn't crying but more like howling. I was scared. I had never heard her make a noise like that. I jumped up into her lap and curled up, hoping that might help. She stroked my fur and said, "He's gone Scamp. Just gone. And no one was with him. He was all alone." And then the terrible sounds began again.

It got dark and still she sat there with me in her lap. Later that same evening she started making phone calls. She sat on the couch with a box of kleenex in her lap and made one call after another to people with different names written down in a little brown address book.

When we got in bed that night she stroked my fur and said, "I don't know what I'd do without you Scamp. I don't think I could survive this without you."

She was gone for several days and when she came back I sensed that something had changed in her. For a time it seemed as though she didn't care about much of anything. She stopped going out and some days she never got up, just stayed in bed reading and eating chocolates. That suited me just fine as I loved being curled up beside her. I napped and she read. It was a perfect arrangement.

One day some strange men arrived in a small truck and started unloading ladders and buckets of paint. They didn't speak english and I couldn't understand what they were saying, but they painted the house inside and out. I stayed out of their way.

After that other strangers arrived and carpets were cleaned and new drapes were hung and flowers were planted on either side of the brick walkway leading up to the house. I did not like all this coming and going and having strange people around at unexpected times. I took to hiding under the bed or going out most of the time.

Finally things calmed down again, but it was a temporary lull. A 'For Sale' sign went up in front of the house and there were more strange people in and out. Fortunately it didn't last long. One night around 9 o'clock the phone rang. I was sitting in M's lap on the little enclosed porch where she watched TV in the evenings. I heard her say, "Yes Shawn. That's wonderful. It's done then." And the next day the 'For Sale' sign had another smaller sign on it that said, 'SOLD.'

After that there were no more strangers and things returned to normal. Only they didn't.

We were moving. M told me two night's later. I was almost asleep and she was stroking my fur and she said, "We're leaving LA Scamp. No reason to stay here now. Scotty's gone and there's nothing for me here now. We're going to go someplace where it's quiet and peaceful and beautiful and you will be very happy and I will heal."

A couple of weeks later the upset started again. M came home from the grocery store with a car full of boxes. That was just the first of many trips to the store for boxes. They were all over the house and she was putting the house in the boxes or so it seemed to me. It was all very strange and I took to staying outdoors for longer and longer periods of time. M seemed very preoccupied and sometimes I don't think she even missed me. But if it got too late she'd call because she never wanted me to be out too late at night. Truthfully I didn't like to be either.

Then came a morning when a very long truck arrived in front of the house. The truck was longer than the house. For the next few hours two men and a woman took everything that was in the house and put it in the truck and then they drove away. M kept me cooped up in the bedroom the whole day. She was afraid that all the activity would scare me and I'd disappear. I almost did when one of the men accidentally opened the door to the bedroom. I got out, but M beat me to the cat door and cornered me under the utility sink and put me back in the bedroom.

That night we slept on the floor on a mattress she borrowed from her next door neighbor. She was very restless during the night and woke me from a sound sleep several times. I understood because I knew something big was going on although I didn't know quite what.

The next morning M dressed and returned the mattress to our neighbor. A cab arrived and she put me in my blue cat carrier and we got in the cab.

"LAX please," M said as she put me on the seat.

The next few hours were difficult and the only reason I got through it was because M was with me.

When we got out of the cab M carried me down a long hallway called a concourse until we came to a place where everything had to be put on a conveyer belt. M handed me, in the cat carrier, to a woman in a uniform while she walked through a doorway called a security gate. On the other side the woman in uniform said to M, "You'll have to take the cat out of the carrier Ma'am."

M said, "If I do that I'll never see my cat again. He's terrified of strange people and places."

"I'm sorry, Ma'am - that's the rules. If you can't do it I'll have to call the Supervisor."

"Well then I guess you'll have to call her because I'm not going to take him out."

I could tell by the tone of M's voice that she meant business. It was the same tone in her voice I heard when she got mad at me for killing a bird.

We waited a few minutes and then I heard a gruff female voice say, "All right what seems to be the problem?"

The 'problem', namely me, was explained with M standing her ground. Then I looked up to see the ugliest human face I think I've ever seen peering into the top of the cat carrier. It looked like a bull dog wearing a visored hat. I drew back as far as I could and lunged upwards spitting as I tried to get out, and away, from this dreadful presence.

I heard the bull dog face say, "All right, all right - just get him out of here." I was hurriedly transferred to M's hand and we moved rapidly down the concourse to our gate. M was muttering curses under her breath and telling me we'd had a narrow escape. I didn't need to be told.

The time on the airplane went quickly enough. I just settled down in the cat carrier and went to sleep. I knew M was near me because I could see her shoes through the slits in the carrier. Every now and then she would lean over and say something reassuring to me.

Once on the ground again I found myself back in a car. My carrier was sitting in the front passenger seat. As soon as we were out of traffic M pulled over and stopped the car. She put her coat in the passenger seat and took me out of the carrier.

"I don't know if this will work Scamp but let's try it. You must be feeling so cramped."

I arched my back, did stretches front and back (M called this my yoga postures which all cats just do), then curled up in her coat and went to sleep.

Two hours later I woke as the car slowed down. Looking out the windshield all I could see were trees - great, tall trees that towered against a very blue sky with fast moving white clouds. It smelled good too. Different altogether from Los Angeles or the plane.

M stopped the car and left me sitting in the passenger seat. When she came back she put me in the carrier, but only long enough to transport me from the car into a house, our new home actually.

M put me down and opened the carrier. I sprang out and sat on the carpet and looked for some place to flee and hide. But there was none.

The room I was in was huge with a very high ceiling and windows in the ceiling which let in a lot of sunlight. The room had a large fireplace and floor to ceiling windows which looked out on a grassy lawn and a dense thicket of trees and shrubs beyond.

"The movers should be here soon," M said, "and you will have to spend the rest of the day in my bathroom." Which is what happened. M made a sign for the bathroom door which said, "Do Not Open - Scared Cat Inside." I had water, food and a litter box. I spent the remainder of the day behind the toilet wishing all this commotion would come to an end.

When M let me out again the furniture from our house in Los Angeles was in our new home. It looked very different and I was a little scared of it until I walked up to the end of the sofa and saw the places where I had used the end of the upholstered arm as a scratching post. I sharpened my claws and M said, "Scamp stop that," and then it seemed as though everything was ok and I wasn't scared anymore.

Over the next few weeks I explored my new world. It was a lot different from the old one. The trees made all the difference. I had never seen so many. We lived in a place called Deer Park which had been built in an old growth forest of Douglas Firs. The houses were quite close together but they seemed so private because of all the trees and bushes. There were a lot of woodlots and these were what I enjoyed the most. I could move silently through the underbrush, smelling smells of mice and voles and damp vegetation. I could sit quietly under a tree bough and observe all that was going on without fear of being seen myself.

It rained a lot but I didn't mind. If I got caught in a rain all I had to do was find a thick bush and hide under it while I waited out the storm. Usually though, at the first sign of rain I headed for home and M would be waiting for me at the living room door that opened onto the back deck. She couldn't put in a cat door because all the doors were made of metal. Instead she became what she laughingly referred to 'as a doorman for a cat.' If she was home she always let me in, or out, on demand so to speak. I will admit I was quite spoiled in that regard.

M loved the house and the trees and the fact that Deer Park had so much wildlife. We often saw deer and raccoon and sometimes skunks. The deer came in small groups and nibbled whatever vegetation the garden offered. They tended to be very hard on roses so M didn't plant any.

M loved the varieties of bird life too, as did I for different reasons. M liked to sit in the turquoise velvet lay-back chair that came with us from Los Angeles, and watch the birds through her binoculars. She had a book with bird pictures in it and I'd hear her exclaiming, "Scamp - it's a Varied Thrush," or "That's a Rufous Sided Towhee", but it was all the same to me. A bird is a bird once you take the feathers off, which I did, before I ate them.

Life was different in our new home. M was home a lot more for one thing. She would get up in the morning, let me out, make herself coffee and go to her 'office.' There she would sit in front of her computer and make clacking noises until early afternoon. She took breaks as she called them, but often three or four hours of her day were spent that way. She was writing a book. I liked having her home. I liked to come into her 'office' while she was working and lie in front of the floor vent and let the hot air riffle through my fur. If the sun was out I'd lie in a patch of sunlight, stretched out sleepy and content.

Of course it was convenient to have her around to let me in and out too. She complained about it at times - but she did it nontheless.

27

As beautiful as Deer Park was, and as much as M loved living there, I knew it was a hard time for her. There was a sadness about her now that was there all the time. Sometimes she would sob in that heavy, heaving way I had first heard after the phone call in Los Angeles. At those times she would come looking for me. If I was curled asleep in her bathrobe on the end of her bed she would lie down beside me and stroke my fur and I knew that my being there was a comfort to her. She would talk to me about the son who had died and I understood that she believed she had failed him, had not been a good mother to him. I wondered about that because she was certainly a good mother to me.

She went on long walks. On cold, rainy days when she got home she would sometimes light the fire in the living room and put on some music and sit in front of the fire sipping sherry from a tiny crystal glass. I loved those times. I would curl in her lap, or, if she was stretched out on the couch I would stretch out my full length on her legs and she would scratch my tummy.

In the summer she liked to garden and she would sit in a flower border, pulling weeds and planting flowers. She even liked to be outdoors in the rain as long as it wasn't cold. She said she never felt closer to nature than when she gardened in a light drizzle.

She hung bird feeders from the stump of the old Doug Fir in the back garden and in summer she would lie on a chaise under the butterfly bushes watching the humming birds sipping nectar from the long purple blooms. I liked to sit under the bird feeders, my tail twitching, my teeth chattering in anticipation. But I knew better than to try to catch birds while she was around.

I had a large territory in Deer Park. There weren't a lot of other cats around. Had it not been for Old Gray Cat I would have had the place pretty much to myself.

Old Gray Cat was a feral Tom with a lop ear, part of his tail missing and a limp. He was mean and he was a fighter. I encountered him early on because he thought my house and garden were part of his territory. I had to take a stand and let him know he was trespassing. We had our first fight about two weeks after M and I moved in.

After the fight there was a lot of white tummy fur, mine, scattered in clumps in one corner of the lawn. I didn't want to fight him, but he insisted.

The next morning M woke up and said, "Scamp, what's wrong?" I was shaking from head to toe. Waves of shakes. M felt my nose which was medium cold. She put me under the blankets and went to the kitchen to make coffee.

Later that morning I was lying in a patch of sunlight on the living room floor. M was walking from her office to the kitchen and suddenly my hind leg flew up in the air. Straight up, only I didn't do it. Something else seemed to have control of my leg.

M came to me right away and stooping down she said, "Scamper this is not good. You're going to the vet."

I heard her telephoning and when she came back she had the cat carrier with her. I knew what that meant and I didn't like it and I complained, loudly, all the way to the vets.

M had called ahead to explain to the receptionist that I was scared of everyone but her and that I had only been to the vet once before in my life when I was neutered.

When we got there we were put in a room with a very peculiar smell. M opened the cat carrier which was on a high table. When I got out I was trembling all over. M stroked me and talked quietly to me. Soon a door opened and a large man with a quiet voice came and stood by the table and began to run his hands up and down my body, pressing gently hear and there.

"Has he been in any fights lately?"

"Yes he has. Just yesterday in fact, with an old, wild Tom that lives in our area."

"He's got several puncture wounds on his hind legs," the vet said pulling a scab off one and pulling it out of my fur. He did that with all the wounds he could find then stroked me firmly several times. "He's scared isn't he? You'll be all right now Scamp. But you have to stay away from that old Tom."

The vet gave M a prescription of anti-biotic with instructions for how often to give it to me and we went home.

Over the next few days I took the medicine because M forced my mouth open and squirted the nasty stuff down my throat. But I got better.

I had other fights with Old Gray Cat but somehow I managed to hold my own with him so that he understood that he couldn't just barge into my territory without a fight. After a while he got so he wouldn't come through the garden unless he was sure I was in the house.

Other than that I didn't encounter anything threatening in Deer Park. I knew better than to make a raccoon mad, or a skunk, and the deer had no interest in me at all.

Sometimes M went away. When she did an elderly lady who was M's mother would come and stay with me. At first I was scared and hid under the bed or went out. But gradually I became quite used to her and didn't mind having her around. She was really no trouble and she seemed to understand my aloof attitude. Her name was Peggy and she was always very gentle and quiet with me. I liked the fact that, like M, she talked to me. She knew I understood what she was saying.

The first time she came to stay I walked around M's bed meowing. Peggy stood in the doorway and watched me.

"It's all right Scamp. She's only gone for a few days. She'll be home soon."

Since 'soon' didn't mean anything to me I continued to tell her that I missed M and wanted her home.

Peggy went to M's closet and pulled out her bathrobe and put it on the overstuffed chair by M's bed. Then she went away. I waited a while until I heard her making tea in the kitchen and then I jumped on the chair and curled up in the bathrobe. It smelled like M and I felt safe and secure curled up in it. From then on whenever Peggy stayed

31

with me she always put M's bathrobe in the chair for me. I got so comfortable with Peggy that I would even go in the kitchen when she was fixing something to eat and rub against her legs letting her know I was hungry too. Sometimes when Peggy slept in M's bed I would even curl up on the end of it.

I don't think M really understood how hard it was for me for her to be gone, and there was no way for me to tell her. I had no way of knowing if she would ever come back.

As soon as she got out her dark blue suitcase and put it on the bed I knew she was going away. She would talk to me while she packed.

"Scamp," she'd say, "I'm going away on Tuesday. I'll only be gone four days. I'll be home Saturday. Carla will come every day to make sure you have fresh food."

While I understood she was trying to reassure me, the words 'Tuesday' and 'Saturday' meant nothing to me.

When she did return I would act strangely, hiding under the bed, or running outside and standing on the other side of the hedge that separated our house from the house next door and meowing pitifully as though I was lost. When she came outside looking for me and I'd run away from her. She didn't understand this behavior at all, so I decided drastic measures were called for.

The first night after she returned from her next trip I woke her from a sound sleep by rubbing my freezing cold nose (my 'ice cube nose' M called it) along her cheek. Then I lead her to the kitchen and insisted on being fed. That was just a ruse to get her up. When she went back to bed I ran beside her and scratched the top of her foot. I did this several times when she returned from trips. I never drew blood, just left a few harmless scratches as a way of telling her how upset I was.

She didn't think much of this behavior at all. Once I caught her off guard when she got back into bed by jumping in the bed and scratching her shoulder. She picked me up and deposited me in the hallway outside her bedroom and shut the door.

I heard her saying from the other side of the door, "That's enough of that young man."

But I got the better of that argument. There was a small space between the bottom of her bedroom door and the carpet. I slid my paw under the door and rattled it. It made a very satisfactory noise. I didn't have to rattle very long. She opened the door, picked me up, tossed me on the bed and said, "All right -you win - now settle down." Which I did quite happily.

We lived in Deer Park for four years and they were the happiest years of my life. M rigged up boxes beneath her bedroom window so I could come and go at will for much of the year. I was always in at night although I devised a little game just to prove who had the upper hand. I'd hear her call, but I wouldn't come until I saw her bedroom light go out. I'd wait until I was pretty sure she was asleep then I'd run up on the deck. She'd hear my collar tags and sleepily make her way through the dark living room to let me in, grumbling about how naughty I was not to come when she called me.

Sometimes M would say to me, "Scamp - I don't know how much longer we can afford to live here." I wasn't sure exactly what that meant, but something about her tone of voice warned me that a change might be coming.

Then something happened which made change inevitable. M had put an ad in the local paper advertising for someone to share the house with. She got several phone calls and I heard her asking callers questions over the phone, but only a couple of people, both men, came to the house to look at the room.

Then one night after we were in bed asleep the phone rang. M answered it sleepily, and as soon as she heard the callers voice her voice got very tight and I knew she was afraid. I heard her say, "No I'm not interested and please don't call again." She listened for a moment longer and I thought I heard a man laughing when she hung up the phone.

She lay down again but I knew she was scared, very scared. Her body was stiff and I could smell her fear. We lay for a long time, but I don't think either one of us was asleep. I must have dozed off though because the next thing I knew my whole body was catapulted straight up in the air, my fur standing up on my back and tail. My claws, which were fully extended, raked M's arm as I shot upwards. I bounced on the floor, then back onto the bed, my legs stiff as pokers. I don't know whether I was dreaming, or whether something I heard or smelled scared me. I don't know. Poor M. I left big bloody scratch marks on the underside of her arm when I shot into the air. She got up and went to the bathroom and I heard the water running. She came back and got in bed and stroked me over and over saying, "It's all right Scamp. It's all right. We're going to be ok."

The next day she looked terrible and I felt terrible about the scratch marks. But she wasn't mad at me at all. She knew we'd both been scared out of our wits.

Later that week M told me she'd found a place for us to move to. She said that I'd like it because there were empty feed lots close by where I could hunt mice to my hearts content.

So we went through the whole process of putting the house into boxes again. Several weeks later two men and a truck pulled up and started loading all the boxes and the furniture and I had to spend another day in the bathroom.

I was not happy to be moving. I loved Deer Park. I was very content there and I couldn't understand why we had to leave. But leave we did. For the first two months in the new place I spent most of my time under M's bedspread. She would come and sit on the floor and look under the bedspread and talk to me.

"Scamp, come on, get up. You can't go on like this forever." But I could and did until one fine day she picked me up like a newborn kitten and carried me out to the patio off the living room. She put me down on the cement and she said, "There. Now get a life."

That was all very well for her to say, but it wasn't so easy. I missed the wood lots and the wildlife of Deer Park. I missed my old territory and I even missed Old Gray Cat.

But there were compensating factors. I discovered that another cat lived next door. A young female who was put out in the morning when her owner left, and not allowed back in again until her owner came home. I thought this was pretty awful because M had always made it possible for me to be in or out depending on my wishes. I realized how lucky I was.

I enjoyed my relationship with 'kitty' - that was her name, she had no other - and began to look forward to going outside again every day. I had never had a relationship with anyone of my own species and I found I really enjoyed the companionship. We played chase under the cedar trees that grew on a small embankment behind the house. Or we would sit side by side under the boughs and enjoy the feel of the spring sunshine on our coats. Sometimes we'd go hunting for mice in the feed lot across the street.

That summer M had company. I liked to sit at the end of the hall and look into the living room. The company would see me sitting there and comment to M.

"There's Scamper. Come on out Scamp. Don't be scared. I love cats." I never worked up the nerve to actually let a guest pet me, but I would run into the living room as though the hounds of hell were after me and stand nervously by the sliding glass door until M, laughing at me for being so silly, would open the door and let me out.

M's company slept on a couch bed in the living room and that didn't suit me at all as it meant I had to move fast and hope the sliding glass door was open.

The night of August 24th was not unusual in any way except that the moon was full and very large as it lay low on the horizon. I had been in M's bedroom until she got ready to go to bed. Then I asked to be let out. It was a warm night and she left the sliding glass door open so I could get back in again whenever I was ready to come to bed.

36

Later that night I slipped into the house, past the guest asleep in the living room and made my way down the hall to M's bedroom. I wanted to be under the covers so I used my ice cube nose and nudged her cheek to wake her just enough to lift the covers so I could go underneath. I snuggled down close to her and tried to go to sleep, but found I was restless. It seemed to me that the moon and the soft night were restless too, and that I was wanted outside. I made my way out from under the bedclothes and felt M's fingers brush my side gently as I moved past her sleeping head on the pillow.

I made my way up the hall, past the sleeping guest, and stood in the opening of the sliding glass door, smelling the night smells. Mouse was what I had on my mind and I knew just where to find them. Moving quickly in anticipation I slipped outside. The cool night breeze felt wonderful on my coat. I skirted the neighbor's yard and crossed the street to the feed lot where I ducked under the pipe pole fence. I stopped and listened to the sounds of the night. I could hear a soft rustling in the tall grasses which told me there were mice nearby. Life was good and the full moon gave a silvery patina to everything it touched.

# Spirit: Don't Fence Me In

# "Don't Fence Me In"

I was an adorable kitten. Everybody said so. I am a standard American short hair tabby, gray with black stripes and a white blaze down my nose, white paws and tummy. My most distinctive features, are the symmetrical black tiger stripes on my front legs, and the black tufts on the ends of my ears. 'M' says they make me look like a lynx - whatever that is.

Since I was so cute I found it surprising, and a bit disturbing, that when Tanya handed me to 'M', who was meeting me for the first time, 'M' was crying. It was only later that I understood why.

I was born in a ceramic shop, in a comfy box under the counter. My mother belonged to the shop owner. Since the owner was eager to find good homes for me and my three siblings, she encouraged her customers, women of all ages, to play with us. I got the most handling because, as I have already said, I was so cute.

One day a pretty young woman with long blond hair came into the shop to get a pop from the machine. When she looked in the box where my mother and we four lay snuggled together asleep she asked the owner if she could take me back to her workplace to show me to one of her co-workers.

Tanya picked me up and snuggled me under her coat and we left the shop and went into the office next door. She stood in front of the reception desk and spoke to someone I couldn't see.

"Look what I've got," she said, taking me out of her coat and holding me over the desk. The woman behind the desk didn't say anything. She just sat there looking at me as I dangled over the desktop. I looked at her and 'meowed' as I wasn't crazy about my precarious position. Then I saw the tears in the woman's eyes and finally, she reached out to me and took me in her hands. She held me close and stroked my fur while the tears continued to roll down her face.

"This is a very strange reaction," I thought to myself. "Why would she cry when I'm so cute?"

Tanya handed the woman a kleenex and she wiped the tears away.

"Is it a she or a he?" she asked.

"It's a she I think," Tanya replied. "She's one of four born to the cat next door in Pam's shop."

"Is Pam selling them?"

"No. I think she just wants to find good homes for them," Tanya said.

"She's too little to wean yet, but tell Pam I'll take her in a couple of months if that's ok."

Tanya returned me to my mother in the box under the counter and over the next two months my siblings disappeared one by one until I was the only one left. The woman from next door came to see me almost every day and I soon came to look forward to her visits. I noticed that at first she seemed very sad, but something about being with me, murmuring nonsense words and nuzzling her nose in my fur seemed to help her so that by the time she went back to work she looked happier.

It got very cold and rainy and fewer people came to the shop. I had the run of the place and liked to hunt mice at night and play on the tables during the day where people were making bowls and plates. This was not always a welcome activity because sometimes I'd roll an instrument they were using off the table and bat it around on the floor.

One evening just before closing time the woman from next door came into the shop carrying a blue cat carrier.

"I'll take her home with me tonight Pam if that's all right," she said.

"That's fine. I think you'll really enjoy her. She has such a sweet spirit," Pam said.

"That's it. That's what I'll call her. Spirit," the woman said smiling at Pam as she scooped me into the carrier.

She put the carrier into the back seat of her car and we drove for quite a while until we got to a place the woman said was 'home.'

'Home' was very different from the ceramic shop. For one thing it was a lot smaller. After snooping into every possible corner I decided that it was going to be quite satisfactory except for one thing. That one thing lay behind a large sliding glass door and a plate glass window. It was called 'outside.' From the first moment I noticed it I was fascinated by what lay beyond the glass - a veritable fairy land of wonderful and surprising things - grass, trees, birds, insects, smells, flowers, sky, wind. I couldn't wait to get beyond the glass. Unfortunately it was not to be. My new owner let me know from the very first day that I was to be what she called 'an inside cat.' What this meant was I could never venture beyond the limits of the small duplex in which we lived. That first winter the only time I was outside was the overnite I spent at the vets when I got spayed.

Nice as my new home was it was much too confining for me and over the course of the next few months I planned and executed several aborted escapes. It was winter and cold so 'M' didn't go out the sliding glass door very often, but when she did I tried to sneak out hoping she wouldn't notice.

After one of these attempts 'M' picked me up and marched me down the hall to her bedroom. My heart was beating very fast because I knew my escape attempts annoyed her. She sat down on the bed with me in her lap and got a framed photo from the bedside table.

"Look Spirit. Isn't he handsome? His name is," she paused and gave a small sigh, "was, Scamper. He loved to be outdoors and I let him out whenever he wanted. He went out one full moon night and he never came back. That's why you can't go outside. I can't go through that again."

I looked at the photo of a handsome male tabby with markings so like my own and thought to myself that he could have been my father. Something about the sadness in 'M's' voice reminded me of her tears the first time she saw me and I understood why she had cried when Tanya held me out to her.

I decided I couldn't give up my hope of going outdoors. I would simply have to be patient, but it was hard. Sometimes I simply couldn't stand being cooped up and I would run, ears back, tail humped up, down the hall, into the living room, around the dining room and back up the hall to the bedroom. I would carome off the furniture, streaking up the backs of chairs, and shinnying up the wicker bookcase in M's bedroom. M would laugh and tell me to 'get down at once - you look like one of the bad kittens in Beatrix Potter's "Tale of Tom Kitten." ' But I had to do something to use my energy. Lying around all day snoozing is for old cats, and I was barely out of kittenhood.

Sometimes out of pure boredom I would play a game with 'M'. For a while it became a daily event. Every morning she would remove the foil wrapper from her teabag and crumple it up, tearing it along the bottom and making it stick up like a tail. She would throw it in the air and say, "Get the mouse Spirit." I would leap into the air, catch the 'mouse', bat it around the kitchen then drop it at her feet. It was our version of fetch. The game seemed to delight 'M'. I enjoyed it, but it was no substitute for 'outside.'

Then one early spring day I was sitting behind the blinds that shuttered the sliding glass door watching birds at the feeder. 'M' must not have seen me because next thing I knew the door was sliding towards me on the track and I saw 'M' step out onto the patio. So quick she didn't have time to slam the door shut I was outside. There was a row of small cedar trees planted on a low embankment right behind the cement patio. I dashed under the nearest cedar with 'M' in hot pursuit behind me. Fearing that she would capture me I looked about for another hiding place. In an open field behind our garden stood a lone Doug Fir, quite tall, with a bare trunk. I streaked out from under the cedar tree and made for the Doug Fir and climbed up as far as I could go until I was spread eagled on the trunk about seven feet high. I couldn't go any further and I was afraid to let go and drop. 'M' stood behind me laughing, her hands on her hips.

"Come down from there at once you bad cat," she said. But I couldn't move. She approached the tree slowly and just as she got to it I retracted my claws and dropped like a stone into the grass below. 'M' reached down and scooped me up and carried me wriggling back to the house.

It wasn't much, but it was a beginning. I had been to that wonderful, magical place - outside. I couldn't wait to do it again. It was at about this time that I began to behave in a way that 'M' found disturbing and strange. I would walk around the house meowing. That's all, but it was enough to dismay 'M'.

"What's wrong with you Spirit? Why are you acting like such a goof?"

If cats could yell I would have yelled. I just had to hope she would get the message eventually.

I was lying on the back of the couch looking out the big living room window at the birds one day when 'M' sat down beside me. She sat stroking my coat, watching me watch the birds.

"You'd like to be out there wouldn't you girl?" she said very softly.

In response I chattered my teeth and twitched my tail.

"Well maybe it can be arranged," she said, leaving me wondering what she meant.

Not long after on a day of lovely spring sunshine a man came to the house. He and 'M' stood on the patio talking and gesturing while I watched them from the back of the couch. As he was leaving I heard 'M' say, "I think it's worth a try. She's so determined to get out I hate to keep her cooped up." I knew she must be talking about me.

The man came back soon after and began using a big metal stick that he screwed into the ground. He kept hitting rocks which caused him to swear and I could tell he was not enjoying what he was doing. He dug holes from the fence to the corner behind the cedar trees, then more holes behind the cedars and then up the other side of the back yard. I watched his every move from the back of the couch. Something was afoot, but what I didn't know.

A few days later the man appeared carrying big rolls of something I subsequently learned was called chicken wire. He put a metal post in every hole he'd dug and then he began attaching the chicken wire to the posts. I noticed that the chicken wire flopped over at the top about a foot. None of this made any sense to me. Still, it was interesting to have something new going on in the garden. It provided me with a little relief from the boredom of my days and I was grateful for it.

'M' and the man would confer frequently and one day as he was leaving I heard her say, "We won't really know if it's going to work until I let her out."

Who out? Me? Who else could she mean but me. I was so excited I began pacing and meowing.

"Spirit just be patient. It won't be much longer now."

The next day the man appeared again, this time carrying long pieces of lumber. He disappeared around the side of the house and soon there were sounds of hammering and sawing. He was at it a long time, but he finally called for 'M' who went to look at whatever it was he was building. When they came back 'M' said, "I'm going to let her out and see what happens."

'M' opened the sliding glass door behind which I had been sitting patiently for what seemed like hours. I looked at her, pricked up my ears and stepped eagerly onto the patio. I was sure with that move that 'M' would be on me and I bounded across the cement and the small strip of lawn and scooted under the lower limbs of a cedar where I hoped 'M' wouldn't be able to see me. She just stood there laughing and said to the man, "I think she thinks I'm going to chase her." When she didn't move I slipped quietly under the boughs of the neighboring cedar. It was lovely under there, cool and secret. I could see out, but I was sure nothing could see in. A bird fluttered to a branch overhead and I crouched down, my teeth chattering and considered how best to reach it. It was about five feet over my head towards the top of the tree. A small, red breasted finch. Before I could develop a strategy it flew away. Then I heard 'M's voice very nearby. "She's hiding under the lower branches," she said to the man. "She thinks I don't see her." The next thing I knew 'M's arm was coming at me. I raced out from under the cedar and around the side of the house and there stood the explanation for the earlier hammering and sawing - a stout wooden gate about 7' high. I didn't think I could scale it so I turned my attention to the chicken wire fence. It looked flimsy and there was a foot of the stuff hanging inwards which would make it difficult to get over. I decided to capitulate and without further fuss I rolled over on my back and wriggled in the grass. 'M' squatted down beside me and rubbed my tummy and then, to my complete amazement she got up and walked away leaving me there, tummy exposed to the lovely spring sunshine.

That was the beginnng of my life 'outside.' The cedars were really the only place in the garden to hide and so they became my cave. I would lie under the lowest boughs and watch what went on. There were birds a-plenty. 'M' had hung a bird feeder and it attracted song sparrows, finches, pine siskins and the occasional rufous-sided towhees who liked to peck at the seed hulls on the ground under the feeder. I caught many a bird that summer and would frequently bring them into the house if 'M' had left the sliding glass door open for me. She'd hear the commotion in the living room and she would come running and insist I drop the bird. Then she'd put me in her bedroom and close the door while she went back to the living room to try to rescue the poor creature. Sometimes it was dead, but sometimes it was just stunned and then 'M' would take it out front and put it under a tree. She always gave me hell for this behavior, but I think she also knew that it's just what cats do and for us it's perfectly normal behavior as well as survival.

The summer passed peacefully and I spent as much time as possible outside. 'M' always made me come in when it began to get dark, but I didn't mind that as long as I had the freedom to be outside as much as I wanted during the day. 'Outside' was just as I'd imagined it and even better. The variety of sights, sounds, smells and experiences was delightful. I thought about trying to get over the fence or the gate from time to time, but I wasn't at all sure it was possible.

Then one day, quite by accident I discovered an escape route. I was climbing up the trunk of the cedar closest to the fence that separated our duplex from the one next door. I was after a siskin sitting on a branch a few feet above my head. I'd gotten almost up to where the bird was when it suddenly took flight. I was annoyed, but not too surprised. This happened with regularity. I was clinging to the trunk and about to go back down when I looked across the fence and saw that the cedar boughs from the tree on the other side of the fence were lying on top of the chicken wire. Without another thought I leapt to the nearest bough and ran along the top of it and presto - I was on the other side of the fence. I scrambled down the cedar trunk and dropped to the ground - my heart beating very fast. Now I was really outside. The most outside I had ever been in my life. I half expected to hear 'M' in hot pursuit behind me, but after crouching at the base of the tree for several minutes it became clear she was unaware I had escaped. I moved slowly under the cedar trees in the neighbors yard and then made my way into the tall grasses in the field behind the duplex. This was new territory. I had never experienced anything like it. I knew I was hidden by the grass so I took my time, walking slowly and stopping every so often to listen and smell. There was a small breeze blowing and on it I could smell all sorts of delicious things - mice, moles, birds, something pungent but unidentifiable. There was a sound too that I had heard before but never been able to identify. It was a loud noise, and insistent as though the creature making it was vexed about something or demanding something. The noise was growing louder as I moved in its direction. "Mack, mack, mack." The ground underfoot became damp and suddenly I was in a grove of very tall trees. In front of me was a pond with birds I had never seen before floating on it. Every now and then one of these creatures would stand up in the water beating its wings and making the 'mack, mack' sound. I crouched down in the grass fascinated. I had never seen a pond before, nor the birds and all I wanted to do was to stay there in the shade of the great trees, watching.

Then I became aware of a distant voice. "Spirit." It was 'M'. She had discovered my disappearance. I couldn't see her or the duplex, but I knew from the sound of her voice that she was anxious about me. Fearing dire consequences if I didn't let her know I was all right I made my way back through the field and emerged onto the back lawn of the neighbors' yard. When 'M' saw me she came to the fence, a worried frown on her face.

"Spirit how did you get out? Get back in here right now." It didn't take her long to figure out my escape route and she cut back the limbs of the cedars on both sides of the fence.

The rest of the summer became a never ending contest between the two of us to see who could outwit whom. I discovered that by shinnying up the metal posts I could get over the fence, and, as I had grown bigger and stronger I was now able to jump to the top of the wood gate as well. 'M' was hyper vigilant and managed to round me up before I had gone very far, but by the end of summer almost all the fence and the top of the gate was festooned with rolls of chicken wire. One day she was showing a woman friend the 'cat fence' as she called it and the woman looked around and said, "Hmmm - kitty Dachau." I could tell from the look on 'M's face that she was not amused.

But the thing that upset 'M' the most was those occasions when I decided not to come in at night. I didn't do it that often and then only as a way of showing her how determined I was to have my freedom. She would watch TV, calling me periodically, and I just wouldn't come. I could hear the anxiety escalating in her voice as it got to be bedtime. Finally, I would see the living room light go out, she would call me one more time, and then she'd go to bed. But she'd get up during the night, and call me from the sliding glass door. I might be just a few feet away from her under a cedar, but she'd never know it. Usually by the second time she'd call I'd had enough and would come bounding across the patio and into the house, up the hall and onto her bed. She'd rub her face in my cold fur all the while scolding me, and then we'd both go to sleep.

On a couple of occasions I stayed out all night - just to prove I could. Her reaction puzzled me. She would appear the next morning looking haggard and old, and something else. Resigned. As though she expected it and even knowing how much it would hurt to lose me, accepting it. I would feel very badly that I had caused her such misery and I would be unusually loving and affectionate - for a couple of days anyway.

But I continued to escape. It infuriated her and altho I felt sorry for her I wasn't about to give up. I didn't just want 'out' I wanted my freedom - complete and unfettered. That shouldn't have been so hard for her to understand, but I guess it was.

One day something so unexpected happened that I think it caused her, finally, to give up the fight. I caught a bird and 'M' rescued it and it flew across the fence to the neighbor's garden where it sat a few feet away in the grass. With 'M' standing right there I took off at a run and went right **through** the fence. I could hear M gasp and say, "I don't believe it. That's not possible." 'M' squatted down and began to examine the chicken wire. After going carefully over the mesh she found a slit, not visible to any eyes but mine, about a foot off the ground and several inches long. 'M' stood looking at it for quite a while then she said, "I'll bet the yard man did it with the weed whacker."

She disappeared into the house and returned with a pair of wire cutters and some wire. She mended the slit with the wire then she cut a small hole, just big enough for me, right through the chicken wire at ground level. I knew then that our war of wills was over. She had finally capitulated.

Not long after I had achieved complete freedom to come and go at will so to speak I had an experience that helped me understand why 'M' was so protective of me. I had gone to the duck pond early one morning and was sitting, hidden by tall grasses bordering the pond, calculating how I was going to get me a duck. Several were within a few feet of the edge of the pond and I was concentrating very hard on them when I became aware that I wasn't alone. A creature that looked very like a dog was creeping towards me. It was a yellow-brown color, with very large triangular ears and long skinny legs. It too was stalking the ducks but something told me it would just as happily stalk me.

I took off running towards home with the creature in hot pursuit. I knew I wouldn't be able to get in the sliding glass door because 'M' always closes it after she lets me out in the morning. And I wasn't sure the back yard would be safe so I streaked around to the front of the duplex and went as high in the ornamental plum tree as I could go. The creature stood on its hind legs and appeared to be about to shinny up the trunk after me. Instead it thought better of it and ran around the base of the trunk sniffling and whining. Then it disappeared. I stayed in the top of the tree, scared out of my wits. I had no doubt whatever that the creature would gladly have made a meal of me. I knew sooner or later 'M' would get up and call me so I waited until I heard her calling from the sliding glass door. When I didn't come she waited a while, called again and when I still didn't appear she opened the front door and stood on the steps calling. I scrambled down the trunk and tore in the front door, my tail humped up, my ears flat and my fur fluffed out like a Hallowe'en cat.

"Spirit. What's the matter. It's me. Come here and tell me what scared you."

By this time I was under her bed determined never to come out again - ever. 'M' went about her business and I could hear her bustling in the kitchen, but I stayed under the bed. Finally hunger got the better of me and I emerged and made my way down the hall to my food dishes. 'M' watched me eat and when I'd finished she picked me up and carried me to the lay back chair. For once I didn't protest and try to wriggle out of her arms. She sat me in her lap and stroked me.

"What happened girl? Why were you up the plum tree? Was it a coyote?" Her hand stroking my fur felt very good and I began to relax.

"I tried to tell you Spirit. It's why I didn't want you running loose around here. You've got to be careful because there are coyotes around all the time - even though we live in town. They are very clever. You never see them. Just all of a sudden people start missing their cats and sometimes dogs too - if they're small. You must promise me you'll be careful - especially towards evening and early morning."

Our lives have fallen into a predictable pattern. Most mornings I wake her around 6:30 by gently placing my paw (no claws) on her cheek. She will open one eye and then, grumbling, get up to let me out. Some mornings I stop at my food dish and sit beside it looking expectantly up at her. She knows this means I want some moist food. She'll put some in my dish and I'll eat a few mouthfuls and then I'll ask to be let out.

It's summer now and the days are very long. I alternate my time between hunting and killing birds and mice, and snoozing under the cedars or between the mattress pads on the chaise lounge. And I still visit the duck pond even though the ducks are gone until fall. It's like being in the woods - full of a secret and wonderful life where something is always happening.

In the winter months I spend much more time indoors because it's often cold and rainy and I'm happier inside snuggled on my blanket on the couch or asleep on the poof on the end of 'M's bed. When she's working on the computer I like to go into her office and make a nest out of the paper in the large wastebasket under the computer table. I curl up in it and go to sleep to the sound of the computer keys going clack-clack.

All things considered I can't complain. I think I have the best of both worlds – hers and mine. 'M' and I seem to have reached an accommodation. She understands and respects my need to be free; and I understand and respect her desire to keep me safe. We both know that loving each other involves a certain amount of risk, but one worth taking.

# Berry Picking

# BERRY PICKING

Memory is funny stuff. Sometimes it's there when you least expect it. Other times when you need it most it eludes you. Memories may be the only thing we take with us when we 'shuffle off this mortal coil' for memories are uniquely ours, they belong to nothing and no one else in the Universe.

Mine came unbidden the other day while I was picking berries. It was a perfect day for it, overcast and just cool enough to be comfortable. I had driven to Graysmarsh Farm a few days before to find out what sort of equipment was needed and I came prepared with plastic bowls and old Cool Whip cartons to put the berries in. I parked and walked with my bowls to the stand where a matronly woman assigned me to row thirty-three. Never having picked commercially grown berries before I asked if I should move to the next row higher or lower after I had picked row thirty-three. The woman just smiled and said for me to come ask her knowing far better than I that the chance that I would pick an entire row was practically nil.

I found row thirty-three and put my containers down a few yards from the end of the row and began picking. I quickly discovered that like everything else in life there is a certain rhythm and technique to picking raspberries. If you squeeze gently at the top of the berry, pulling down as you squeeze, the ripe berry will slide off its white cone with almost no resistance. Sometimes berries fell into my hand just from having been jostled as they sat, waiting on their vines.

One of the chief delights of berry picking is eating the berries as you go. The vines were so laden with ripe berries that finding them was no problem. Eating them became the problem and I had to discipline myself to eat one only every now and then for fear I would get a stomach ache. I tried to clean an area before moving on and even went so far as to squat down on my haunches in order to pick the berries at the lower elevations.

I was grateful for the cloud cover even though it obscured the peaks of the Olympics in the distance. Even with the heavy bank of gray cloud the nearer mountains could be seen above the long vista of rows of vines. It was a lovely, peaceful sight and it made me feel as though I had been transported to another world. None of the frantic press of human activity which most of us take for granted even as we profess to detest it intruded here. For now there was only one thing to do and I moved slowly and quietly down the row absorbed in finding and removing the sweet, dark red globules and putting them in the container or my mouth.

I could hear people talking to each other in nearby rows and found myself eavesdropping on a discussion of family matters being conducted in the row next to mine by an older woman of definite opinions and two younger ones who had mastered the knack of setting her up and off. They moved more quickly than I and soon left me behind. I don't know at what point I first heard the birds, but they had been there all along and I had just been too intent on my task to notice. Once I did hear them I found it difficult to shut them out of awareness. They were shore birds, gathered in the marshland bordering the fields where the vines grew and for which Graysmarsh Farm is named. From the decibel level and the variety of honks, bleeps, whistles and toots that comprised the concatenation I concluded there must be a very large number of them. I had a sudden hankering to go find them, but I knew that Graysmarsh Farm does not allow anyone to walk its beaches and marshes for recreation. Still, the rules couldn't stop me from hearing the birds and they added significantly to the pleasure of the day.

I'm not certain when in the progress of the morning I found myself thinking of my step-father, but I suddenly became aware that I was. He was always pleased at any sign of housewifery in me and picking berries in a field in order to make jam would have been an undertaking that would have had his full cooperation and approval. I wondered about that and decided that it had to do with Bill's childhood in Pendleton, Indiana. He was raised on a small farm owned by his grandparents, both of whom had been slaves. He loved his Grandmother who was a strong, proud woman who feared God but no man. She had a root cellar into which she put the farm's bounty in the form of canned vegetables and preserves of all sorts, including I'm sure, raspberry jam. Bill's childhood stories always included vivid descriptions of his Grandmother's cooking. He himself loved to eat and appreciated the alchemy required to transform simple foods into delightful surprises for the palate.

I knew that he would have approved of me standing there among the raspberry vines on the edge of the continent under a gray sky. I don't think of him often and when I do it is not always with affection.

He was a difficult man and the complexities and tangles in the triangle composed of him, my mother and myself often made relating to him uncomfortable. Nontheless, I know he loved me and was proud of me and in truth, in the thirty-two years he and my mother were married he brought me as close as I will ever come to having a father, and my children a grandfather, and for that I am grateful.

As I said, memory is funny stuff. It would never have occurred to me that while picking raspberries on the Olympic Peninsula I would remember my step-father.

# The Cows

# THE COWS

I woke up that late summer August morning to the sound of cows. Not the occasional moos to which I was accustomed. But rather a constant cacophony of disturbed loud noise emanating from many bovine throats.

Cows were one of the chief things I loved about living in this small farming community on the Olympic Peninsula. Cows had been among my first, and happiest surprises when I, a total stranger to these parts, found myself living here after forty years in Los Angeles.

The town itself was small; only about 1500 people lived within its limits. The area was growing though and in process of transition from the dairy farming community it had once been to a home for those like me, retiring from life in the big city. There had once been many herds of prize dairy cows in the area. Now there were few. Federal government regulations imposed on dairy farmers in the 70's meant outlays of capital few farmers possessed and many simply sold their herds then sold their farms to the developers. Some, angered at the loss of a means of livelihood and a way of life they loved, sold their dairy cows and replaced them with small herds of beef cattle. These were primarily what remained in the area surrounding the town, and these were what I heard bellowing in alarm that morning when I awoke.

My duplex was on the edge of town. The north side of the street a block away was still part of a working farm and I could walk through the stubble of an open field to an electric fence that kept the cattle contained in a pasture. It was one of the things that had first appealed to me when I was looking for a place to live. As I drove up the street looking for the address the rental agency had given me I noticed the cows crowded near a gate in a pipe rail fence. They were waiting for someone to feed them. The fact that they were there, so close, was not distressing to me at all. I knew that there would be times when I would smell them and hear them as well as see them and that suited me just fine.

I rented the duplex and was not sorry. It was perfect for my needs which consisted primarily of a room to write in and peace and quiet. The living room windows and sliding glass doors were at the back facing what the British call 'waste ground.' I subsequently discovered that it had been the railway right of way, long abandoned and now simply a stretch of open ground that grew up into waist high grasses in the summer and was a brown stubble in winter. Out of the sliding glass doors in the back I had a view of the Olympics which, in winter, with snow on their peaks, was magic. They were less imposing in summer without their frosting of pristine white. Behind a cement patio there was an embankment planted with young cedar trees. In the summer I sowed wild flowers and enjoyed their haphazard colors against the evergreen of the cedars. The living room had a small fireplace and on rainy winter days I could light a pressed log and lie reading or listening to music, my cat Spirit stretched out on my legs with a look on her face of utter contentment.

The cows were not obtrusive in any way. I liked to cross the field and stand as close to the electric fence as I dared get to watch them when they were pastured near the house. They were a mix of black cows, which I took to be Black Angus, and red ones which may have been Herefords, but I wasn't sure. The young calves were fun. They would chase each other in a way that to me seemed playful and they also seemed less wary than their elders. They would take tentative steps towards me curious to know what I was. The adult cows on the other hand were clearly more fearful. They would lower their heads and snort and then, like as not, bolt taking their calf with them. I noticed that many of them had red ear tags with numbers on them and asked a friend, more knowledgeable about cows than I, what the tag meant. He said, "That means they've been sold." "For meat?" I asked. "Yes," he said.

I discovered I really didn't want to know that particular piece of information. It disturbed my vision of the bucolic peace and quiet of my chosen home. Like most city dwellers who move to the country I was in love with the landscape. The realities of a farming way of life with its hardship and never ending chores, its smells and muck and dangers was not something I really cared to confront. It was enough to drive through miles of fertile land under cultivation, to enjoy the pleasure of peaceful vistas of pasture lands where cows and horses grazed.

But sometimes, standing watching the small herd, smelling the strong, sweet pungent smell that accompanies all cows the red tags and the truth of their meaning would intrude on my happiness. That truth was, quite simply, that the animal I was looking at would die, or rather be killed, to feed me. I pondered that and could find no way out of or around it. There was, in fact, no other purpose, no other meaning, to the four footed life before me than that simple truth. Try though I might, I could not avoid it. As a single woman, living alone, I am not much of a meat eater. But I do like it. A tender filet mignon, or a good brisket - there's nothing like it. The truth is - I am a carnivore. I not only like meat, I seem to crave protein. I have tried diets which eliminate meat altogether (and what 20th century woman hasn't tried at least one such diet in her quest for the perfect figure), and they make me feel weak and faint.

The reality is that although in principle I believe we all ought to be vegetarians thus eliminating the necessity for killing other creatures, in fact I am a long way from being able to realize that principle in my own life. This being true I feel hypocritical preaching the desirability of a vegan diet to others. But standing in the pasture close to the creatures whose lives would one day nourish my own I found myself feeling guilty and wishing there was some way out of the dilemma that did not involve a complete change of lifestyle. For someone born and raised in the U.S. eating meat is a cultural 'given.' The vast majority of us do it. The very economy of the region I so love is based in large part on just that fact. The farmer whose 'beef' I was looking at standing there in the pasture was not raising it so I could enjoy living in proximity to cows. It mattered not at all to him that I enjoyed waking at night and hearing a cow 'moo.' He raised cows for one purpose only. To sell them. Did he too not have a right to his lifestyle? Cows served a very different purpose in his scheme of things and yet, his purpose and mine were not as far apart as I liked to believe. He raised them. I ate them. And in between a lot of people depended on that basic fact for their livelihoods. Try though I would, standing there watching the black cow switch her tail while her calf butted its head at her teats, I could not escape that simple fact.

The morning I awoke to hear the fearful racket of the herd I wondered what on earth had stirred them up. I threw on some clothes and dashed out of the house and around the corner. A cattle truck was backed through the gate in the pipe rail fence into a holding pen where the herd milled. The smell of cows was strong in the air. Two men, one bare chested although the morning was cloudy and a bit chill, were attempting to get the cows up a metal ramp and into the truck.

The men were yelling and waving their arms as they chased the animals. The cows, frightened and confused, rolled their eyes as they dashed in different directions unused to having the calm order of their lives disturbed in this way. Finally one of the red cows, her calf by her side, started up the ramp. Other cows pushed up the ramp behind her. But she stopped just short of the door seeming to have thought better of it. She turned and tried to force her way through the cows now massed behind her. The cows stood packed together, unmoving. Finally the bare chested man yelled at his partner who was closest to the red cow, "You're gonna have to hit her with your stick." Both men were holding sticks that looked like dowels about two feet long. The man whacked the red cow on her head and she turned slowly and made her way back up the ramp and into the cavernous recess of the truck her hooves making a hollow metalic sound on the floor. The others followed without protest.

It didn't take long for the men to get the truck loaded and finally they closed the rear doors and went and got in the cab. All I could see of the cows now was the dark outline of their ears through the slats at the top of the truck. It was eerily silent and I realized that they had stopped mooing.

The truck drove up the street and out of sight around the corner and I was aware of stillness and silence leaving me with a strange feeling of emptiness. The birds, normally busy and noisy at this time of day, seemed to have disappeared. There was no one on the street but me. The quiet seemed unnatural and then it came to me - it was the stillness of death.

# A Thanksgiving Memory

# A THANKSGIVING MEMORY

## Margot Fritz

Someone, I'm not sure who, once said: Life is what happens to us while we're busy making other plans. I had the truth of that brought home to me quite graphically over the recent Thanksgiving holiday.

I had gone to Vancouver, Washington to be with my son Adam, his fiance, Kris, and my two granddaughters, Chelsea, 13 and Hillary, 10. Adam and Kris were celebrating their first Thanksgiving in their own home, a brand new two story house in a pleasant development of similar homes.

Thanksgiving was observed in the traditional way with turkey and stuffing. As usual the turkey took about two hours longer to cook than anticipated, but no one seemed to mind and it was worth the wait.

The following day Adam and Kris, both employees of QFC, went off to work leaving Grandma in charge.

I had already decided I would take the girls to Ft. Vancouver, so, after a late breakfast and a leisurely morning we took off for the Army post on which the restored fort is located. The girls grumbled. "Why do we have to go? Couldn't we go to the mall?" I replied that the day after Thanksgiving is the busiest shopping day of the year and I had no intention of getting caught up in it.

Once we got to the Fort and joined the guided tour of the old buildings they seemed to enjoy themselves. I found it fascinating to see how life was lived in 1845 under the strict protectorship of the Hudson's Bay Company factor, John McGlaughlin.

By two o'clock when the tour ended the girls were hungry and we decided to head for the nearest Subway sandwich shop. I was driving down Mill Plain Boulevard when from the back seat ten year old Hillary said, "Grandma, my finger's stuck in the seat belt."

I am chagrined to confess I laughed, as did Chelsea. "Well get it out Hillary," I said. "What a silly thing to do."

A short time later I could hear the anxiety escalating in Hillary's voice.

"Grandma I mean it, I can't get my finger out and I'm scared."

Sighing at the ridiculousness of it all, I pulled onto a side street, got out of the car and opened the back door.

Hillary held out her hand. The flat metal plate that fits into the buckle was jammed over the knuckle of the ring finger of her right hand. The finger was already red and beginning to swell.

Think, I said to myself. Think. I crossed the street and knocked on the door of a nearby house. When a man appeared I briefly explained the situation and requested a bowl of water and some liquid soap. He closed the door and returned shortly bearing my requests, then trailed me silently as I returned to the car.

But it was to no avail. Not all the soap in the world was going to unwedge that metal plate.

"There's a hospital just a quarter of a mile up Mill Plain. You better take her to emergency," the man said.

I returned his dish and soap, thanked him and drove off. In the back seat Hillary was growing fearful.

"They're not going to amputate my finger are they Grandma?" she wanted to know.

"No darling. That won't be necessary. They'll cut the plate off."

In the front seat, elder sister Chelsea offered the information that they would undoubtedly use a ring cutter, and further ventured the opinion that her sister was mentally defective for jamming her finger into the stupid thing in the first place.

A wail arose from Hillary in the back seat. "I'm the stupidest person alive," she howled. "Daddy's going to be so mad."

I tried to sound reassuring as I pulled into a handicap parking space directly across from the ER entrance to the hospital. I left Chelsea in the car with her sister and ran into the ER. A quick scan of the lobby entrance told me I had picked the wrong day for this. The place was mobbed. People in wheelchairs, an elderly man having his blood pressure taken by the woman behind the admitting desk, a woman with a crying baby and an assortment of people with ills I didn't have time to catalog.

A green coated technician leaned towards me from the other side of the admitting counter.

"Can I help you ma'am?"

"I hope so. My ten year old granddaughter is in the back seat of my car with her finger stuck in the seat belt."

Quicker than you can say ER I had two green coated techs on either side of me walking me out to the car. They got in the back seat with Hillary, one on either side of her, and looked the situation over. Then, using liberal applications of KY jelly they attempted to remove the metal plate from her finger. It didn't budge. Using a knife-like implement one tech cut the fabric part of the belt and all five of us trooped into the ER.

Both technicians seemed to be in accord that this was a simple matter which could be taken care of without the necessity of going through a formal admitting process. One of the techs went to find a ring cutter while I waited with Hillary at the admitting desk. The tech re-appeared with the implement and he and the other technician attempted to cut through the metal. Seat belts are not rings and the metal refused to yield. At this point the two men realized they had exhausted their resources and that more drastic measures would be needed.

The next thing I knew we were in an examining room and I was becoming more than a little concerned. It was at the point that someone entered and clipped a plastic ID tape to Hillary's wrist that it ceased being an inconvenient situation that could be easily remedied and began to assume the proportions of a medical emergency. All sorts of horrendous scenarios were playing in my head. Hillary too was becoming more apprehensive.

Before long a stocky man with a bushy brown beard and wearing a white coat appeared. He was a doctor.

"Well young lady," he said looking at Hillary's hand, the silver metal encasing her ring finger. "You're making getting engaged a little difficult aren't you?"

"No. It's the wrong finger," Hillary replied, not sure she liked this attempt at humour.

"Oh, so it is. Well let's see what we can do about this."

The doctor gave the technician some instructions which included obtaining gauze, 'mosquito scissors' and ice. Within a few moments an orderly appeared holding a green cotton cap like the ones worn in surgery, only this one was filled with ice.

"I want you to keep this around your finger and keep that hand up. Ok?"

Hillary did as she was told, but her apprehension got the best of her and, her blue eyes as round as saucers, she had to ask again, "You're not going to amputate my finger are you?"

"No. Nothing so drastic as that" the doctor asssured her.

While Hillary lay on the examining table, her arm elevated and her hand thrust into the makeshift ice bag a young woman in street clothes appeared with a large clip board and began asking the usual questions.

"Patient's name?"

"Her age?"

"Her address?"

I got through the first two, but realized I didn't have the remotest idea what the address of the house was, and what was worse I didn't have it written down anywhere. I silently kicked myself for being so haphazard as to go driving around a strange city without knowing where 'home' was. Hillary didn't know the address either.

"Date of birth?"

Now I was really feeling remiss. What kind of grandma doesn't know her own grandchild's birth date? Fortunately Hillary came to my rescue.

"January 16th, 1989."

I was astounded that not one question was asked about insurance. I volunteered the information that Hillary's Dad had insurance coverage and that I knew she was covered as his dependent. In this age of horror stories about the callousness of some aspects of the medical establishment, I found it laudable that the primary concern on the part of all the hospital staff, from start to finish, was the welfare of the child.

I asked the woman to stay with Hillary while I went out to the lobby to find Chelsea and tell her we'd be a while yet.

Soon after I returned to the examining room the doctor reappeared with one of the technicians.

"Well let's see what's going on here," the doctor said.

He examined the finger, then wrapped it very tightly with a thin gauze bandage. When he had wrapped it down to the metal he asked for a strip of rubber used as a tourniquet when blood is taken. He wrapped that tightly over the gauze. Only the tip end of Hillary's finger extended beyond the bandage and it was a dark purple.

"Ok Hillary. We're going to let that stay that way for a few minutes. That wrapping will reduce the fluid in the end of your finger and then we'll be able to get that silly thing off."

The doctor and the technician left the room again and Hillary and I waited. Time as we normally know it stops when you're going through something like that. It becomes time out of time - surreal.

At one point Hillary became upset and began to cry and ask for her Daddy. I ducked out the door and collared the first staff person I saw and requested that someone call my son at his store. I would have done it myself, but I felt I needed to stay with Hillary.

The doctor returned and I had the feeling that the serious part of this whole episode was about to begin. I was right. After removing the tourniquet and the gauze and applying KY jelly the doctor, using his thumb and forefinger on either side of the metal began to rock the plate gently from side to side in order to work it up Hillary's finger.

It began to hurt and she began to cry and call for her father. All I could do was hold her other hand and try to find words that would soothe her. When the doctor had worked the plate up to the knuckle the pain increased and Hillary began to rock her head from side to side and kick her feet up and down on the table.

My granddaughter is made of tough stuff. She never once said, "No." She never once said, "Stop." She did not try to bat the doctor's hands away or remove her hand from his.

The doctor was the essence of cool. As concerned as I was for Hillary and the pain she was in, I was aware of the doctor as well. He appeared to be totally focused on working the plate slowly up her finger with a slow, rocking motion.

Suddenly, Hillary, her voice almost a whisper said, "I felt it move." And then I knew it was going to be all right. There were a few more seconds of bad pain for her and suddenly her finger was free and we were both crying and holding each other and I was telling her over and over what a good girl she was and how proud I was of her. The doctor patted her head as he handed her the buckle before leaving the room. It was only a short time later than my son appeared in the open door, his face reflecting his worry and fear.

And so it ended happily with all of us going out for dinner at a local restaurant. Hillary started her dinner off with cocoa topped with whipped cream and then couldn't get through her meal. But never mind. If she'd wanted caviar I'd have been inclined to provide it.

Later that evening watching the two girls sitting in front of the fire locked into an intense game of "Sorry", I thought about the day's events.

I don't know what, if any, significance it will have for Hillary. She said she'd tell the story of the Thanksgiving she got her finger stuck in the seat belt and had to go to the ER.

For me the thing that matters - that I will cherish - is that if it had to happen, it was I who was there for her.

I would never have planned such a thing. I was on my way to the 'Sub' shop. It was life that had other plans.

# The Baby Shower

# THE BABY SHOWER

I had called to ask directions. "At the STOP at the end of town - you turn left and it's the blue house on the corner, across from the Museum."

That was helpful as far as it went, but it didn't get me there from Sequim, I realized belatedly as I hung up. I would just have to consult a map, something I am always a little reluctant to do if there is someone I can ask.

Here on the Olympic Peninsula it is very easy for the unwary newcomer to take a wrong turn and end up someplace they don't expect to be - like Chimacum.

As it turned out the road I took was delightful. It was March and the rolling farmland was covered in the most delicious green, serving as a perfect backdrop for brown and black cattle grazing as they moved slowly in the fading light. I slowed up and let my eyes sweep from one side of the road to the other, enjoying the vistas that unfolded on either side.

Once I had passed over the Little Quilcene River bridge it was a simple matter to find the house. It was indeed blue. I parked in the grass by the chain link fence and entered the house through the garage. An old green carpet scattered with wood chips lay on the floor. A woodpile stood stacked against the back wall.

A little girl of about five, with straight brown hair cut in a bob, was standing in the door leading to the service porch. "The baby's not here yet," she announced with authority. "Melody is late."

"Well," I replied, "that's how it is when you're a Mommy. You're always late for everything."

The child held the door and followed me into the kitchen. Four young women were fixing plates of food - crab puffs, small quiches, bowls of M and M's - peanut and plain.

There was no formal greeting. I announced who I was and one of the women, who identified herself as Jennifer, said, "Kat said you were coming. You called for directions didn't you?" I said I had and that ended the discussion. No introductions were made. The other three women were busy putting the plates of food on a long table covered by a white cloth. A sheet cake with red roses piped in each corner proclaimed, "Welcome Meaghan."

I did not feel ignored. The complete lack of formality, of ritual observance of the niceties of polite behavior, was in a way more comfortable than what I was used to. I went through another small room and into the living room which contained a couch and several large chairs and a television set, which was on. I put my purse and jacket down and seated myself. There were several young children running around who would occasionally come into the living room, stare at the TV for a few seconds and run off again.

The house was shabby. Every piece of furniture looked as though it was long past whatever prime it might once have enjoyed. A ceiling fixture cast a light that was harsh and indifferent over everything below. There was no attempt at interior decor. Furniture was placed where it was based solely on utility.

The young woman who had introduced herself as Jennifer came into the living room with two large spools of pink and white crepe paper. She unwound two long pieces and began twisting them together. She was quite heavy and I watched with trepidation while she heaved herself onto the arm of the couch. I went to help her by handing her the scotch tape, and to be of assistance should she fall. She balanced neatly against the wall to steady herself and using the piece of scotch tape I handed her she stuck the streamers to the wall. That done she executed a similar operation in the opposite corner.

Suddenly there was an excited yell from the little girl who had originally greeted me. "The baby's here. Melody's coming." An exodus of children occurred and there was a commotion in the kitchen area as mothers and children swirled around a dark-haired young woman carrying a baby carrier covered by a pink blanket. Behind her, and protectively close to her, was a well muscled young man with a crew cut. The baby had arrived.

Now the whole tenor of the evening changed. Melody, the new mother, settled herself on the couch, the baby in her arms. The older children ranged themselves on either side and in front of her. All the children wanted to see the baby. Not all of them wanted to hold her. Those that did took turns sitting beside Melody, and she in turn, would place the baby in their young arms. The children were fascinated by her tiny hands. One child wanted only to rub the back of his knuckles gently over her head and cheeks. I never heard a reproof to 'be careful,' or 'don't do that' from Melody. The baby was asleep and unconcerned with the attention she was receiving.

By now the room was nearly full and one of the young women who had been in the kitchen when I first arrived was bringing presents into the living room and piling them on the floor in front of Melody. I greeted Doris, the baby's great grandmother, who had lived up the street from me years ago in Los Angeles. Her boys and mine played together and her daughter Katherine, always called 'Kat', baby sat my children. The family had moved away to a place called the Olympic Peninsula many years before, but our youngest sons had kept in touch and remained friends. At the time the thought that I too would one day live on the Olympic Peninsula would have seemed the unlikeliest thing imaginable.

Doris is a tall, large woman. For years now she has had a condition which makes talking difficult and her voice is raspy as though she is constantly in danger of losing it altogether. Doris is devoutly religious and when you talk to her you have the sense that all of her life experience is filtered through her intense belief in God. Her life has not been easy, but faith has sustained her through many difficulties: an alcoholic husband, a son with a debilitating illness, and a beloved niece murdered in her early teens. But those burdens were clearly lifted as I watched her cradle her first great-grandchild in her arms.

Kat, Doris' daughter, dressed in tight jeans and a square- necked cotton knit shirt, squatted down in front of me, a big grin on her face. Her slim body belies her forty plus years but the hard won battle she fought with alcoholism shows clearly in her face. There is a quality about Kat, a certain gutsiness, that makes it clear that she is very much her own person, whatever her frailties may be.

Looking up at me, her hands on my knees, Kat said, "Would you ever have believed it?"

"Never," I replied. "Not in a million years. The least likely thing I could ever have imagined. But I'm so glad I'm here." This last was a reference both to the fact that after forty years in Los Angeles I now live on the Olympic Peninsula as well as to my presence at the shower.

The tears started to my eyes and Kat squeezed my knees and rose to go sit beside her daughter and grandchild and her mother on the couch. Looking at the tableau before me I realized that I was looking at four generations.

By now the small rooms were crowded with people, adults, both men and women, as well as all the children. I had asked earlier when Jennifer and I were working on the crepe streamers how the children were related and it appeared that many of them were nieces and nephews of the new father. His mother and father were there as well.

The living room seemed to be exclusively the domain of the women. The men hovered in the doorway of the kitchen, close enough to see what was going on, but with enough distance from the event so they could not be said to be actually participating in it. Showers, after all, are for women. Not even women's lib seems to have affected that.

I asked Melody if I could hold the baby and she handed her to me without hesitation so she could turn her attention to the huge pile of gifts which now covered much of the living room floor.

And so I sat, a newborn cradled asleep in my arms, for nearly an hour. For most of the time I seemed to be in some dream place. I heard the din of adult exclamations over the beauty, originality or utility of each gift, the babble of the younger children (there were by now at least two more infants on the premises as well) and none of it seemed to penetrate the sacred space I occupied. I was alone with the child sleeping peacefully in my arms. Occasionally one or another of the children would approach and peer intently over the edge of the blanket that enveloped the sleeping infant. They would reach inside the blanket and pull out a tiny hand and wonder at it before letting it go.

The baby began to stretch, its fingers balled into fists, its legs pushing against my side indicating it was no longer asleep. She made some snuffing sounds, and one or two choked cries, but never really came out with a solid bawl. Then she lapsed back into the private world of sleep for several minutes before the stretching and pushing with her legs began again.

As always I marveled at the strength in a newborn. They can push against you in a most determined way making it very clear that they have something on their minds from which they cannot be deterred. After several of these displays it was clear she was seeking her mother. Melody collected her from me and asked her husband to change the baby - a task that was eventually performed by the grandmother to spare the father the embarrassment of having to minister to the baby in front of a roomful of women. That done, she was returned to Melody who, with no embarrassment whatever, nursed the baby while the children watched, their faces solemn.

I rose and stretched and suddenly realized I was hungry. I left the living room and went into the kitchen where most of the men were hanging out. Nobody had announced that food was being served or available but it was clear from the half empty plates that people had been helping themselves so I did likewise.

Two men and an attractive blonde were standing in the doorway discussing an event that involved police. The woman was saying: "He comes up to me and he says, 'I know who you are. I've heard all about you from Buddy.' Yeah. Well. So that tells me everything I need to know."

The stocky young man facing her said, "Hell, he don't even know Buddy. He's always making out he knows something he don't." I returned to the living room to discover that the deep swivel rocker I had been sitting in had been co-opted by one of the mothers who was bouncing a baby in her lap. I perched on the arm of another swivel rocker, the only available seat as the room was now crowded to capacity.

The young woman who was sitting in the rocker got up and said, "You can have my place, I'm leaving now." I thanked her and sank gratefully into the plush contours of the chair. Before me the pile of presents had dwindled to one huge box that had clearly been saved to the end.

Leaning over to run her fingernail between the box bottom and the lid to sever the scotch tape holding the two together, Melody pulled what appeared to be a quilt from the box's interior. She stood holding one end while someone else held the other corner to display the quilt to the room. Someone next to me murmured, "Darlin did that for her. That girl can cross stitch like nobody's business. She did all that by hand."

It was a large quilt. Too big for a baby's crib. It was white with a red border of cross stitch and in red cross stitched letters it said, "Meaghan Baker, March 7th, 1998."

Everybody seemed pleased. This then was a fitting finale to the shower. It seems everybody knew Darlin was making it so there was a proprietary pride in the finished product now revealed to the new mother for the first time.

Melody, smiling broadly said, "I knew when you called and asked how to spell the baby's name. I thought, oh no, she's making me a quilt." But she was clearly pleased and I felt that for her the quilt was a given, a tradition that confirmed her child in the culture of the small community where she was born.

Driving home in the dark, on quiet roads empty of traffic, I reflected on what I had just experienced. A shower may seem like a frivolous thing, but it is not. It is about the continuity of generations, it is about past and future and ultimately it is about welcoming a new life to the planet.

Most showers are held a month or two before the baby is born. I prefer it the other way. There is something wonderful about having the person being honored there - not in utero - there, crying, sleeping, to be handed from one pair of arms to another, to be marveled over by the children, and to say by its very presence, "I am here. These are my people. I belong."

# AUTHOR'S COVER BIO

## Margot Fritz

Margot Fritz was born in 1933. Her professional career included four years' employment for the County of Los Angeles as a social worker, and 22 years working in the world of non-profit programs. She has been Director of Training and Executive Director for a national child abuse program and a fund-raiser for AIDS and homeless programs. She is the mother of three, divorced, and currently living on the Olympic Peninsula where she is working on a novel. Cats have been an important part of her life since early childhood. Her current cat companion, Spirit, is the subject of the story, "Don't Fence Me In".

# ABOUT THE ARTIST

Pat Taynton's portraits of animals, both wild and domesticated, have been exhibited in galleries in the United States and abroad. The Franklin Mint, the World Wildlife fund, Defenders of Wildlife, the Jacques Cousteau Society and the National Wildlife Federation have all commissioned her work. She presently lives and works on the Olympic Peninsula and can be reached at: 360/681-4432.

New
PA

Printed in the United States
1052400004B/314